I'm 78!

(and Counting!)

Poems for Perky Pensioners

Joyce

First published in Great Britain in 2022

Copyright © Joyce Warrell 2022

Cover illustrations by Joyce.

The moral right of the author
has been asserted.

All rights reserved.

No part of this publication may be
reproduced, stored in a retrieval system,
or transmitted, in any form, by any means,
without the prior permission of the author,
nor be otherwise circulated in any form of
binding or cover other than which it
is published and without a similar condition
being imposed on the subsequent purchaser.

*A huge thank you to
all of my dear family and to my lovely friends
who have continually encouraged and inspired me
to write my rhymes
and to even dare publish them!*

Joyce x

CONTENTS

PART I – I'm 78!

I'm 78!	2
My Tapestry	3
A Stout Stick	4
Why?	6
Me!	7
My Brain	8
Life	10
Ironing	12
The Washing Line	13
The Compost Bin	14
Autumn	16
Up to Me	17
Technology and Me	18
The Dentist	20
My Shower	21
The Postman	22
Sleep!	24
Wheee!	26

Isolation at our House	28
Isolation Week Two	30
Our World	32
What Day is it?	33
Topsy Turvey	34
Thank You!	36
The Chelsea Pensioner	37
I'm only Human	38
The Snail	40
Captains of our Ships	41
The Highland Cattle	42

PART II – I'm 79!

I'm 79!	46
Poohsticks	47
A Cornish Pasty	48
I Love Books!	50
On and On	52
Armistice Day	54
Leaves	56
Duvet Day	57
The Funny Side!	58

Sprouts	60
A Simple Christmas	61
My Bobble Hat	62
Digging Deep	63
January 1st 2021	64
I Love my Car!	65
A Strange Result	66
Being Positive	68
Holding On	70
A Waiting Game	72
The Olive Tree	74
I'm Coping, I Think!	75
Screenplay	76
That's it!	78
Hope	80
Brisk	82
Meandering	83
Two Sides to Every Story	84
Hot Water	86
A Spring in my Step	88
As Old as you Feel	89
Deliveries	90
In Search of Laughter	92

It's Magic!	94
Touch Wood	95
A Switchback Ride	96
Housework	98
Itchy Feet!	99
My Hairdresser	100
Upcycling!	102
Gardeners	104
Daisies	106

PART III – I'm 80!

It's never too late!	108
A Gold Star!!!	109
Marital Bliss	110
Catching Leaves	112
Autumn	113
Senior Moments	114
Colours	116
Socks!!!	118
Tough!	120
An Uncertain World	121
Whistling!	122

Crackers!	123
The Magic of Christmas	124
My New Year Resolution	126
Toilet Humour	127
All of a Twist!	128
Funny Habits	130
A Silver Lining	132
Dining with Friends	134
Sweet Peas	136
Shades of Green	137
Stuck!	138
Bring Me Sunshine!	140
Phones!!!	142
Lambs!!!	145
A Moment in the Sun	146
The Beach	148
Help!!!	150
Feet!!	152
Spiders!	154
Pets	156
Saying Goodbye	159
About the Author	160

PART I

I'm 78!

"A smile is a curve that sets everything straight"

Phyllis Diller

I'm 78!

I'm 78 how can that be?
Inside I'm only 23!
Time has flown - no GALLOPED by!
So many things I want to try.
So many things I haven't seen
and places I have never been.

BUT

I'm ALIVE and functioning!
And I've got time to notice things
like spiders' webs and butterfly wings,
and I can TALK and smile and sing!

SO

I will cherish every day
and take whatever comes my way
and if I never get to Delhi –
well I can visit on the telly!

My Tapestry

When I look back upon my life
it's like a tapestry,
with interwoven colours,
threads and jewels for me to see.
Some dark, some dull, some shining bright
- and each a memory
of all the many things
that have been happening to me.

It's great that all the darkest colours
seem to fade away.
The brightest colours seem to shine
and glow more every day.
The FAMILY times, the special times,
the happy times, the friends.
I'll keep sewing my tapestry
with COLOURS 'til it ends.

A Stout Stick

Most days when I walk along
I'm looking at the ground.
I'm watching where I put my feet,
no time to look around.
But now my Geoff has found for me
a stout and sturdy stick!
He found a branch, just lying there
all knobbly and thick.
We brought it home,
he smoothed it down, and cut it to my size
and now a whole world's opened up
before my very eyes!

I'm feeling safe and confident
and I can STRIDE along!
I can't believe that I've been looking
downward for so long.
I see the patterns in the sky,
the sun, the trees, the birds,
I see the beauty all around
and I am lost for words.

And LIFE, I think, is just like this
– it's great to have support.
A partner, family or friend

– it's such a simple thought.
We ALL need help along the way
– (well if you're just like me)
So as I travel through my life
that's what I'LL try to be,

A STOUT STICK!

Why?

Have you ever wondered why
a plane will stay up in the sky?
Why ocean liners stay afloat,
just like any smaller boat?
Why flies can always see you coming?
Why bumblebees and wasps keep humming?
How DO birds produce their feathers?
Why do we have different weathers?
How can plants grow from tiny seeds?
How can colds travel in a sneeze?
Why does the moon shine every night
then disappear when it's daylight?
How rainbows form. How do birds sing?
I wonder about EVERYTHING.

BUT

When I puzzle over those,
I ask my grandson and
HE KNOWS!

ME!

Does everybody feel like me?
Fit as a fiddle! Fit as a flea!
Able to climb the tallest tree!
Able to swim in the coldest sea?

Well YOU will know - it's all inside!
I'm getting older - had my ride.
My joints are stiff. My back is bent.
My hearing kind of upped and went.
I stumble when I walk along.
Sometimes my words all come out wrong.
My eyes don't see well any longer –
my glasses keep on getting stronger –

BUT

In my MIND I'm twenty-three!
Fit as a fiddle! Fit as a flea!

THAT'S ME!

My Brain

My brain is like a space ship.
It's full of knobs & switches!
Sometimes it's working perfectly
and sometimes there are glitches!

It's funny how a word I want
can sometimes disappear
then later on it pops back in,
shining bright and clear.

It's funny how, when I was young,
I sometimes learned by rote
and now that I am ancient,
I have to write a note.

It's funny how my specs and keys
just never can be found
and then I find they've put themselves
somewhere safe and sound!

It's funny how I wander out
then have to go back in
to stand and think 'whatever was it
I was meant to bring?'

It's funny how I can't remember
where I put my purse,
my phone, my bag, my credit card?
Oh help! I'm getting worse!

BUT!

I'VE found the solution
to mend the faulty wiring!
I write a host of Post-it notes!

ALL CYLINDERS NOW FIRING!

Life

Life is such a precious thing.
It's watching birds fly on the wing.
It's listening to children sing.
It's seeing an old lady grin!

It's making most of every day.
It's taking joy from games we play.
It's splashing on a rainy day.
It's feeling warmth in the sun's ray.

It's respecting your fellow man.
It's giving all a helping hand.
It's caring when you visit gran.
It's loving whenever you can.

Life is hard and sometimes mad!
It's PEOPLE who can make me glad.
A cuppa cheers me when I'm sad
and friends are precious when life's bad.

It's difficult when getting old.
Your joints ache and you feel the cold
BUT all your stories can be told
and memories are made of gold!

So when my legs just feel like lead
and I can't even leave my bed,
I'll look back on the life I've led
and STILL be dancing in my head!

Ironing

I've got a pile of ironing.
It's growing every day.
I'll have to do it soon
because it's getting in my way.
It's collars that I hate the most.
They drive me round the bend.
No matter how I steam them flat,
 they curl up at the ends.
And then there are the fitted sheets,
I iron the middle flat
but when the corners come around ...
 well I can't cope with that!
And trousers,
what a struggle to get the perfect seam.
I fold and straighten, fold and press.
They make me want to scream!

But TV helps me on my way.
I take a lengthy peek
then put the iron away and SMILE.
That's it until next week!

The Washing Line

There's nothing like a washing line
with sheets and towels all blowing.
A sunny, windy day in March
and all around, things growing.
It fills my heart with hope and joy,
this washing on the line.
Tonight my bed will smell of Spring!
As long as it stays fine!

The Compost Bin

Everyone should have one.
They don't take up much space.
It could live behind the garage.
You'll surely find a place.
And you can compost ANYTHING,
except for wood and weeds.
(A garden full of bindweed?
Not what anybody needs!)

But all the veggie peelings,
tea bags and eggshells too
and torn up bits of paper,
it all goes in the brew.
And dead heads from the roses
and discarded carrot fronds
and old leaves and grass cuttings,
the bin's where it belongs.

It's funny but there's always room
to add some more on top.
I keep on piling it all in
and never seem to stop.
And magic happens in that bin,
it keeps on rotting down
and then in spring there's COMPOST!
All rich, crumbly and brown.

I don't know how it happens.
A miracle occurs!
I really love my compost bin.
(But I'm glad that it's outdoors!)

Autumn

I love the sound a chestnut shell makes
when it hits the ground
and safe inside, a shiny conker,
big and fat and round.
I love the way the acorns fit
so snugly in their cups
and sweet chestnuts that prick your fingers
when you pick them up.
I love the way the hazelnuts
are turning green to brown.
I love to try to catch the leaves
before they touch the ground.
But gathering conkers is the best
without a single doubt,
FOR I spread them all around the house
to keep the spiders out!

Up To Me

At the end of the day it is up to me.
I can LIVE my life or simply BE.
I can grumble and moan at how bad I've felt.
I can loudly complain at the hand I've been dealt.
I can wear people down with my endless woes.
I can criticise people and look down my nose.

OR

I can put a big smile all over my face,
be glad I'm alive as I go place to place.
I can cheer people up with a listening ear,
lend my shoulder to cry on when they shed a tear.
I can look out for people much worse off that me
and offer them cake and a nice cup of tea.

I can look UP not down.
I can look OUT not in.
For life is so short and this way
I'LL WIN!

Technology And Me

Chapter One

Today I bought a laptop,
with lots of sound advice
from someone of a different age.
(I'm older, more than twice.)
I'm told I now need Windows 10
to help me on my way.
I don't quite understand it
but I've got it anyway.

Chapter Two

Today a good friend came along
and charged it up for me.
It's really very simple
as far as I can see.
He moved my files and made new ones
and cleared the memory
and now it's all on Laptop Two
and now it's UP TO ME!

Chapter Three

Today ... HELP!

Chapter Four

Today I've signed up for a course
to learn a thing or three
about this strange new laptop
and all that's puzzling me.
I'm feeling proud and confident
for I will surely be
an EXPERT in computer skills
TECHNOLOGY FOR ME!

The Dentist

Why is the dentist so scary?
She's just looking after my teeth!
But whenever I sit in the dentist's chair
I'm trembling like a leaf.
As the chair goes back, I go stiff as a board.
I cross all my fingers and hope
that I don't feel a thing as she peers right in
to give my teeth a poke.

I'll gloss over the next 20 minutes,
pretending that I'm not there.
I'm by a pool on a comfy sun bed
instead of the dentist's chair!

THEN there's reprieve! With a sigh of relief
I thank her profusely and run!
I'm BRAVE and I'm STRONG. I'll burst into song!
and just look at my smile everyone!

My Shower

Each morning when I have my shower
I'm rushing to get it all done.
Get it out of the way. Get on with my day.
I'm planning the things that will come.
I'm washing my hair, going through all my cares
and trying to calm all my fears.
I'm using my soap and I'm trying to hope
that my day won't cause me any tears.

BUT

Today I stood under the shower
and I looked at the water instead.
The droplets so bright
as they shone in the light
and the sounds as they fell on my head.
I watched all the bubbles
dissolve all my troubles,
the drops dribbling down on the tiles.
I felt so refreshed as if I'd had a rest
and I'm facing my day with a smile!

(Live in the moment!)

The Postman

The postman broke our letterbox!
He didn't mean to do it.
But now there's just a slot
and we can see the daylight through it.
But what a brilliant job they do,
delivering our post.
Communication in the way
that I value the most.

Yes, there are bills and junk mail,
flyers and statements too,
but magazines and parcels
and birthday cards come through.
A written note, (so rare these days),
a postcard full of news,
old fashioned ways but ones
that I would never want to lose.

For I can HOLD these messages
and put them on display
and read them time and time again
then store them safe away.
They're treasures for the future,
the memories from my past.
E-mails and texts are brilliant
but they will never last.

So THANK YOU to our postmen
for each delivery.
You bring us more than mail,
you bring much happiness to me.

Sleep!

I've got a lovely cosy bed.
A soft pillow to lay my head.
I'm yawning as I climb the stairs.
I've had my drink. I've said my prayers.
My book's tucked underneath my arm.
(No need to set the old alarm!)
The bathroom next, then snuggle down
and close my eyes. All quiet – no sound.

BUT

Just how DO you get to sleep?
I've spent an hour counting sheep.
I've read my book - so many pages.
I'm still awake – it's taking ages.
I've been downstairs. I've had a snack,
a cup of tea and now I'm back.
I've closed my eyes. Laid down again,
but STILL I can't switch off my brain.

And EVERYTHING goes round my head.
Worries and lists and things I've said
and things I've done and stuff to buy.
I just can't sleep. I wonder why?

YET

Suddenly, another day!
I've somehow slept the night away
and morning's here!

HIP HIP HOORAY!

Wheee!

'Never mind duck' my mum used to say
'It'll all come right in the end.
Let's do what we can to lighten life's span
even though we've no money to spend.
We can go for a walk.
We can sit down and talk.
We can make ourselves nice cups of tea.
We can play in the park,
try the swings for a lark
or skim down the slide with a WHEEE!

We can skip and play ball
and when friends come to call
we can share a jam sandwich or two.
YES! When I was young, life was so much fun,
there was always so much we could DO!
It's so hard today to tear us away
from the laptop, the phone or TV.
Yes, those were the days,
when everyone PLAYED
and slid down life's slide with a WHEEE!

LOCKDOWN!

"When you reach the end of your rope tie a knot in it and hang on."

Thomas Jefferson

Isolation At Our House

It's weird this time we're living through
and I don't like it much!
I want to fling my arms around
the ones I love, and TOUCH!
I want to see my friends, have fun,
share wine & cups of tea.
Instead I'm isolated and now it's down to me!

SO

We've got to keep our peckers up
and this is what we'll do.
We're going to make a daily list of things
to see us through.
We'll build a routine to our day,
all based round drinks and food,
then find some tasks to fill the hours
according to our mood.
Our house will never be as clean.
Our windows will shine bright.
Our clothes will all be neatly ironed.
My cooking a delight!

And when we step outside
the lawn will be immaculate.

No weed will dare to show its head.
We'll even paint the gate!
We've bought ourselves Crème Eggs
and crisps & Werthers, nuts and wine
and crossword puzzles, books to read
and games to pass the time.
Each day I'll cherish one small thing
that's made me smile again.
I'll write it on the calendar
and it will keep me sane.
But best of all we'll stay in touch
with family and friends
through letters, FaceTime, email, phone
until this nightmare ENDS!

STAY SAFE!

Isolation Week Two

I'm down in the dumps
and I've got the grumps
'cos my lifestyle has gone all astray.
It's hard to be cheerful
when I'm feeling tearful,
can't stop myself feeling this way.
We're just two weeks in, but I'm only human
like you and it's so hard to bear.
I know I am blessed
but by now you'll have guessed,
I'm fed up. I can't go anywhere.

BUT

I must pull up my socks
and take all the knocks
and work out just what I CAN do.
I'll devise a routine
with not too much cleaning
(Well maybe a hoover or two).
I can work out to apps,
join the N.H.S. claps.
I can phone up a good friend or three.
I can dance to a tune.
I can see the new moon.
I can even try doing Tai Chi.

I can sing. I can shout.
I can wander about.
I can garden all day if I like.
I can eat all the sweets
and give myself treats.
I can go on Geoff's exercise bike.
We're in difficult times
so I'll keep doing rhymes
'cos I don't want to sit round and mope.
And I had an idea, then gave a big cheer
When I looked out my old skipping rope.

Don't know if I still can but I'll give it a try!

Our World

Could this terrible thing be doing some good
to this Earth where we live? If only we could
learn a lesson from this.
How much we pollute
with our industry, air travel, daily commute!
Venice is CLEAN, its canals running clear.
Our carbon emissions are lowest this year!
50% reduced rate in New York!
We simply MUST sit round the table
and TALK!
Look at the big picture and surely take note.
LOOK, LISTEN and LEARN
is what gets MY vote.
If all our world's scientists gather as one
then saving our world has surely begun!

What Day Is It?

I wake up in the morning
and I feel rather dim!
Is it bridge today or shopping
or going for a swim?
No! None of these!
It's isolation in its umpteenth day.
I've lost all sense of date and time.
I think I've lost my way!
My breakfast's getting later
'cos I read my book in bed.
My lunch is getting earlier
'cos I plan it all ahead.
My evening drink's so tempting
that it's now at four o'clock.
Now, what time's supper?
Oh, I think I've got a mental block!

Bedtime's at ten o'clock these days.
It used to be eleven.
I think before this nightmare ends
I'll be in bed by SEVEN!

Topsy Turvey

My husband found a weed today
and shouted out with glee.
He waved it in the air
and then presented it to me!
We used to hate the weeding,
for everywhere they grew,
But now we find, with their persistence,
we've a job to do!
Today my sparkling window
had caught some pigeon poo.
How satisfying cleaning it
again as good as new.
And yesterday I spilt some milk
over the kitchen floor.
I was so happy mopping up,
I nearly spilt some more!

My world's gone topsy turvey
and chores I used to hate,
I welcome now with open arms,
even anticipate.
I'm seeing things with different eyes
and with a different view.
Perhaps that poor weed WANTS to grow
(and pigeons need to poo!).

So when our world's turned right again,
you'll find a different me.
Considerate and tolerant,
that's what I'll try to be!

Thank You!

As I wake up to start the day,
I think what can I do?
Is there something to pass the time
and stop me feeling blue?
Today I looked around me
and suddenly I knew.
I'd spend my time appreciating
and I'd say THANK YOU!
Thank you for my family
and all the ones I love.
My lovely home so comfortable
it fits me like a glove.
And my dear friends whose company
I once enjoyed so much
and for the new technology
that helps us keep in touch.
The list is never ending,
for everywhere I see
the miracles of nature
and life surrounding me.
For food and drink, my life, my health,
I share this thought with you.
I'm richer than a millionaire
when I stop to say THANK YOU!

The Chelsea Pensioner

The sky was full of clouds today
with not a scrap of blue,
but suddenly they parted and the sun
came shining through.
And lockdown has been just like this,
some sunshine here and there.
A FaceTime with my family.
Phone calls to show we care.
The roses coming into bloom.
A stranger's smiling face.
A new walk or a special meal.
Enjoying our own space.

And then, today, on TV news,
a Chelsea Pensioner.
A twinkly, proud old gentleman
who smiled from ear to ear.
'I've got three meals a day,' he said.
'I sleep in my own bed
and best of all there's no one here
who wants to shoot me dead.'
And I respect that pensioner -
he knows how to survive.
Whatever happens now,
I too am glad to be ALIVE.

I'm Only Human

Inside my head there's a place I dread.
I keep trying to close the door.
But the longer this lockdown
keeps rumbling on,
it's opening more and more.
It's full of despondence.
It's full of despair.
It's full of concern for my family's welfare.
It's full of such longing to see them all soon,
to be with my friends,
for the world to resume,
for no global warming, no Covid 19.
It's full of depression. You see what I mean.

BUT

Inside my head there's a place I love.
I try to keep doors open wide
And the longer this shutdown
is staggering on
I NEED all the things there inside.
It's full of confidence. It's full of hope.
It's full of knowing that we will all cope.
It's valuing family. It's valuing friends.
It's confident this situation will end.

It's full of optimism, full of support,
counting my blessings, positive thought.

When I keep the doors open
to this special place
you'll know that I'm there
by the smile on my face
and to make sure I'm accessing it
more and more,
the first has a padlock,
this one BIFOLD DOORS!

The Snail

The garden snail is not my friend.
He likes to eat my plants.
He glides around my seedlings
munching anything he wants.
And yes, he is intriguing
with his shell upon his back.
It's fascinating when his feelers
suddenly contract.
I like his shiny silver trail meandering along
but still I think my garden's not a place
where he belongs!

I sometimes think in life though,
that I'm a bit like him.
For there have been occasions
when I'VE drawn my feelers in.
I go along quite happily,
then suddenly a blow.
I want to hide inside my shell
while I find a way to go.
And when I'm getting really old,
I hope that I'll look back
and know that through my life
I'VE mostly left a silver track.

Captains of Our Ships

The atmosphere's been stormy.
The seas have all been rough.
It's not all been plain sailing.
In fact it has been tough.
We've steered through many hazards
and faced long days at sea.
We've found the wind to fill our sails,
drunk endless cups of tea.
Good food's been cooked,
we've cleaned and baked,
much wine has passed our lips.
But in spite of all the challenges,
we're still CAPTAINS OF OUR SHIPS!

And now ahead, safe harbour.
Just steer around the rocks.
We'll come ashore to celebrate
when our ships are free to dock!

The Highland Cattle

The first time we walked in the woods near Fleet,
we knew we'd discovered our special retreat.
Woods wrap you in peace,
there's barely a sound
as we follow the paths that meander around.
The trees help us breathe.
They've lived through the years
withstanding this world full of worries and fears.
The fall of a leaf.
The whispering breeze.
It calms us to wander in places like these.

We've listened to birds and we saw a deer,
a doe with her fawn, standing so near,
as still as a statue but watching us pass
then bowing to nibble upon the lush grass.
The greatest surprise we saw through the trees,
a small herd of cattle, just wandering free.
They're huge Highland Cattle,
some with great curved horns,
so slow and so stately in this early morn.
We watched as the big male
just raised up his head
to enable two magpies
clear grubs from his bed.

Today he was scratching his neck on some wood,
in a world of his own.
You could tell it felt good!

In sunshine or rain, when we come away,
we're glad that we walked there
at the start of our day.

PART II

I'm 79!

"No rain, no rainbows"

Hawaiian proverb

I'm 79!

And now I've reached aged 79
and what a year it's been,
for who could have imagined pandemic C19?
And even now it's six months on
the world is still askew
and when it will come right again
we still don't have a clue.
But through the suffering
some good things have risen to the fore.
We're valuing our planet
and the natural world much more.
And we've been given time
to re-evaluate our lives,
take pleasure in the simple things,
slow down ... and we've survived
by doing things like gardening
and learning how to cook
and DIY and making things ... and me?
I WROTE TWO BOOKS!

Poohsticks

Sometimes on my daily walk
I cross a little brook.
Today there was a family there,
they'd stopped to take a look.
And they were playing Poohsticks
and having so much fun.
The little boy was scampering
to see if he had won!
It's always so exciting to see
which stick survives,
and we all know and love it.
We've played it all our lives.
It's being part of nature.
It's simple and it's fun.
(Though it's a bit embarrassing
when you're the only one!)

BUT

Today I have decided,
next time I'll choose two sticks
and see which one's the fastest
and I'LL do it just for kicks!

A Cornish Pasty

Today I ate a pasty, a proper Cornish one
with pastry crimped along the sides
and steak to fill my tum.
And I remembered special times
in Padstow in the sun,
sitting by the harbour wall,
laughing, having fun.
Then I remembered sticky
toffee apples made by Mum,
and sherbet dabs and liquorice sticks
and blowing bubble gum,
and chatting on the corner
after Youth Club eating chips,
three pennorth wrapped in newspaper
with lots of crunchy bits.
And I could go right through my life
remembering great food,
reliving special moments,
recapturing the mood.
I shared this thought with friends one day,
it brought smiles to our faces,
recounting tales of favourite food
and happy times and places.
And now, in lockdown, on the days
when I am feeling bad,

I think of all the wonderful,
amazing food I've had
and as I relive all the times
when food has been involved,
I find that I've stopped feeling sad,
I'm smiling. Problem solved!

I Love Books!

I love to choose another book,
to read the opening page.
I know then whether I'll be bored
or if I'll be engaged.

Is there excitement waiting there?
A gripping story line?
Is it a book I can't put down
no matter what the time?
A book that will transport me
wholly to another world?
A book full of adventures
as the story is unfurled?
A book that will engross me?
Where I can lose myself?
Who knows what magic lies within
that book upon the shelf?

And I can read whilst travelling
by air or land or sea.
(It has to be a proper book,
ebooks are not for me.)
Whilst sunbathing on holiday ...
while curled up by the fire,
relaxing in the garden,
a book's all I require.

And then to read in bed at night ...
it switches off my brain
and stops my worries going round
and round and round again.
For as I read my bedtime book,
I soon begin to doze
and I know it's time to go to sleep
when my book falls on my nose!

On and On

Oh no! Another lockdown
and I am feeling sad.
Somehow when open ended,
lockdown didn't seem so bad
for I could live it day by day
and I could just be me
appreciating different things,
expecting to be free.
This is a different matter,
it will last for 30 days!
So I have made a 4 week plan.
I've had to find more ways!

Week 1 will be the kitchen,
a good deep autumn clean.
The oven can be tackled first
then cupboards in between.

Week 2 the bathroom's calling,
clear any spots of mould.
A miracle for cleaning
is white vinegar I'm told.

Week 3 I'll tackle bedrooms,
sort all the clothes by season.

Week 4 is downstairs left 'til last
for there's a special reason.

December 2nd is the day
we will perhaps be FREE
and we can celebrate
by putting up our Christmas tree!

Armistice Day

Since 1918, Armistice Day
has signalled the end of the war.
Now people could slowly rebuild shattered lives.
There was hope where there was none before.

The ensuing years were hard and austere
but a small price to pay for our peace.
We worked and we prayed
that never again would we fight
and that all war should cease.

But humans are flawed, with ambitious men
who have no compunction or qualms.
Who think they're the best
and despise all the rest.
So once more we took up our arms.

A terrible war. An inhuman war.
A war we remember with sorrow.
For years heroes died, 'til 1945
when at last we could see a tomorrow.

Our heroes then, were regular men,
who fought for the sake of mankind
and our generation have reaped
the rewards of their sacrifice.
But we've been blind.

We've plundered the earth.
We've squandered our wealth.
How stupid and reckless we've been.
We rode hard for a fall,
took our eyes off the ball
and made way for Covid 19.

Our war today is not fought with guns
but with science and brilliant minds.
We're in awe of their talent,
relentlessly seeking a cure
to again save mankind.

And on Armistice Day 2020 the news came
that vaccines were found!
The scientist cried. Their joy unconfined.
The relief of the WORLD was profound.

Now the world holds its breath.
To return to good health is our aim.
Scientists hold the key.
We MUST listen to them.
Do what they advise and build a new future.
AGREED??

Leaves

I was thinking today as I swept up the leaves
that I've never enjoyed it so much.
For always before, it's been a big chore
and one which I don't want to touch.
But lockdown has given a wonderful gift,
the time to slow down and just BE.
And the fresh air, the colours, the physical work
have all become blessings to me.
I've learned to stand still and just look around
and appreciate all I can see.
I've learned not to rush but be there in the moment,
just raking
and lifting
and piling
and touching
and breathing
and happy
THAT'S ME!

Duvet Day

Oh no! It's time to change the bed!
It's such a tiresome day.
I've tried and tried for twenty years
to find an easier way!
It's O K in the summer,
when I can hang it out,
but the cover in the drier?
It all goes up the spout!
I do up all the buttons.
I spread it all around,
but always when the programme ends
it's VERY TIGHTLY WOUND!
Does anybody have a tip?
Something that really works?
I've racked my brains and still I hope
somewhere the answer lurks!
And then to put the cover ON!
It really does take two,
'cos if I struggle on my own
the air sometimes turns blue!

But after all the hassle
when I snuggle down in bed,
I STILL think that my duvet
is the best thing since sliced bread!

The Funny Side!

I had to laugh the other day.
I walked round to my friend's
to hand deliver her Christmas card
as they cost so much to send.
I popped it through her letter box,
of course I wore my mask
but she heard the sound and there she was
with the door open to ask
'How was I? Was I coping?'
It was so great to talk.
Her husband came and there they were,
so glad that I had walked.
But there was such a downpour!
I pulled my hood up tight
and stood there in the pouring rain.
I must have looked a sight!

My furry hood slid down my brow.
My mask disguised my face.
Only my eyes were visible,
an inch the only space.
But do you know me? How we laughed.
It's really me you know!
We really cheered each other up!
I didn't want to go.
It's laughter that will get us through,

it was such a happy chat.
The eyes have it! That is so true
and I'll remember that.

And as I left, still smiling,
I felt a twinge of pride
For even though I'm camouflaged,
well I STILL ME inside!

Sprouts

Sprouts are like marmite,
you hate or adore them
but one thing's for certain,
you just can't ignore them.
They pop up in autumn
and last until spring,
roast dinner without them
is missing something.
Don't freeze them, they're mushy,
but steam them when fresh
and this way you'll taste them
at their very best.
For me they're delicious,
those crunchy green sprouts
but others can't see
what the fuss is about.
So if you are serving them
and I'm your guest
then just have a couple
and I'll have the rest!

A Simple Christmas

This year we'll enjoy a quiet Christmas
with time to reflect what we've done,
for we've all survived this life changing year
which challenged us all, everyone!

We may not unwrap many presents
but the gifts that we have are pure gold.
So, let's all be grateful, enjoy our big platefuls
for we've been allowed to grow OLD!

Have a happy and beautiful Christmas.
Make it one to remember for years.
To all you dear people who enhance our lives,
we're raising a glass to say 'CHEERS!'

My Bobble Hat

I bought myself a bobble hat
to keep me warm and toasty.
I wear it when we go for walks
and it feels good, well mostly,
until today when I was called
a chubby little elf!

WELL

there ARE worse things to be in life
and I am STILL myself!
I'd want to be the kindest sort,
give people lots of fun
and make them laugh and cheer them up
and help out everyone.

SO

NOW I wear my bobble hat
and bounce along and say
to anyone who passes by
'Please have a happy day!'

Digging Deep

An empty house on Boxing Day.
I must get out of bed.
A cup of tea with cranberry toast
will help to clear my head.
Some photos from our family!
A good start to the day.
A country walk in our favourite woods
will help us on our way.
Then home for coffee and hot mince pies
with bubble and squeak for lunch,
a delicious glass of Baileys
to pack an extra punch.
An afternoon of facetime
plus a long zoom call or two,
the TV in the evening,
yes, that's what we will do.

Then Christmas will be over.
Let's look forward to next year.
Let's hope for better things to come
for spring is nearly here
and we'll be out there digging deep
to feed and plant and sow
and all our hearts will fill with hope
as we watch our gardens grow.

January 1st 2021

2021! Here we come!
It will be a wonderful year!
We'll take great strides forward.
We'll regain our lives,
for now the new vaccine is here!
We'll all hug our families,
meet all our friends,
we'll travel and eat great meals out.
We'll go to the cinema,
enjoy a show,
we'll be going out and about!
For we are all stronger (and fitter for some!)
We appreciate all that we've got.
We'll treasure each magical moment this year
for we've learned that we don't need a lot.

AND

We'll say a HUGE thank you to all of the heroes
who've helped us to cope and get through
but TOP of the list are the world's scientists
for we owe our EXISTENCE to you!

I Love my Car!

Oh help! My car's not been out much
but it needs its M.O.T.
It's lived with us for many years
and is getting old you see.
But I love my car and it's become
so much a part of me.
It knows its way around.
(I only drive it locally.)
It fits me and I know it well.
It's automatic too.
I really want to keep my car.
I don't want one brand new.
It's getting a bit battered,
but I don't want for more.
Inside it's warm and cosy
and it makes me feel secure.
So fingers crossed, my little car.
I hope you pass your test.
You're not all sleek and shiny
but to me you are the BEST!

IT PASSED!

A Strange Result

A strange result from Lockdown,
I've discovered where I live!
I never knew the woods around
and the solace they can give.
And there are open spaces
and hills and paths and views
and hidden nooks and crannies
and ALL THESE I can use!

The Basingstoke Canal has towpaths
stretching through the land
and there's even a little brook
very close at hand.
Our town centre is like a hub
and all around is free
to cycle, hike, meander,
(the last applies to me!)

And something always happens.
I giggled I'm afraid
when a young man passing called out 'HEEL',
I instantly obeyed.
I moved behind my husband
to walk in single file.
Of course he meant his dog, not me,
but it really made me smile!

And then an old tree bearing holes,
its branches gaunt and bare
but magical because I think
a woodpecker lives there.

We try to walk early each day,
look for unusual things
and we say 'hello' to everyone
for the happiness it brings.

Being Positive

It's 6 o'clock.
I positively DON'T want to get up
but nature calls
and then I'll go downstairs to make a cup
of tea. I'll bring it back to bed
and have a little read.
Another boring day BUT
I have everything I need.

I'll wear the same old clothes.
I won't be seeing anyone.
BUT perhaps that's for the best,
it's ages since my hair was done.
We'll go out for our daily walk.
Oh no! it's raining hard
BUT never mind, I'll do some housework,
write that birthday card.

Then coffee and some crosswords
and I'll prepare a meal.
Just routine BUT I must accept
that Lockdown is for real.
Then scrabble or a game of bridge,
a glass of wine or two.
Tomorrow is another day.

(ANOTHER to get through!)

BUT yes, at least I'm still alive,
existing in my shell.
I'm lucky that Geoff's with me
and we're both feeling well.

BUT

I'm TIRED of being positive.
I want to scream and shout,
to make the virus go away!
I want to be LET OUT!!

Holding On

On Thursday we got in the car
and went out for the day.
We travelled forty miles or more,
straight down the motorway.
It started raining heavily,
we kept on anyway,
but driving was quite difficult
with traffic causing spray.

At last, we reached the forest
for a welcome cup of tea,
but as I clambered from the car,
I called out "Goodness me!"
For there upon the car's rear door
a snail was clinging tight.
He'd travelled with us all the way.
He must have had a fright!

Through wind and rain,
for many miles,
he'd stayed inside his shell.
He must have wondered
what would happen to him if he fell.
So he'd just kept on holding on.
What a journey he'd been through.

BUT

If a snail can do it
then WE can do it too!

A Waiting Game

I've realised as I've grown old
that life's a waiting game.
As children we can't wait to grow.
Teen years are just the same.
We long for independence,
to make our own decisions.
We just can't wait to join the world,
to find our own positions.

We wait to find a partner.
We wait to have our kids
and we can't wait 'til they leave home!
(Just like our parents did.)
Then we're in our mid-fifties.
We're free to live at last.
We holiday and spoil ourselves,
but soon those years have passed.

And now we're old
we find that we're STILL waiting, for a cure
to eradicate this virus
which is spreading more and more.
But if this Lockdown's taught us all
just one thing then it's this,
STOP WAITING and enjoy the 'now'.
We can't afford to miss

a moment more.
For life is short.
Don't wait your time away.
For we should be so happy
just to LIVE another day.

The Olive Tree

I looked at our great olive tree.
We could be in Spain!
(But when I turn around,
I see the cold and damp and rain.)
Yet with imagination I can recreate the scene
for Andalucía's one of the best places I have been.

I'll stretch out on the sofa.
I'll pour a glass of wine.
I'll read my brand-new paperback.
I'll have a lovely time.
And I'll enjoy an ice cream,
might even wear my hat!
But swimming in the sea or pool?
I can't quite stretch to that!

I'll pass a pleasant hour or two
while waiting for the spring
and, fingers crossed, when summer comes
I'll sample the REAL THING!

I'm Coping, I Think!

Oh goodness, I'm so happy.
We won at bridge today.
It gives me such a boost when things
begin to go my way.
And I STILL look in each long day
for a small bit of cheer.
My calendar since March 20
records them through this YEAR!
It helps to keep me positive
though there's still a way to go,
'cos if I think too much,
that's when the cracks begin to show.

Screenplay

In lockdown we must all agree
technology is KING!
It keeps us fed.
It keeps us well supplied with everything.
We pass the time with playing games
with friends (some socialising)!
We even spend part of our day
with frantic exercising.
Our children take their lessons
and cope with online learning,
and best of all we face time,
zoom and keep communicating.

        BUT

I'm lucky, I don't have to be stuck
to the screen all day.
For many people, it's their work
and they can't get away.
And now it's home school learning,
our children are stuck too.
I feel so sad for them because
I don't know what I'd do.
For when I've spent a morning
concentrating on the screen
I feel disorientated
and I don't know where I've been.

And as I close my laptop down,
I feel all bleary eyed.
I'm dazed and stiff and zombie like.
I feel my brain has fried!
And I am really buzzing
but my body needs some care,
to just feel a bit normal,
I really need fresh air.
I have to go and move about,
to move freely outside.
I need to just be me again,
to open my eyes wide.
To see the world surrounding me,
the spring bulbs breaking through.

YES, we are all technologists
but we are HUMAN too!

That's it!

So that's it.
Lockdown's now till March
and we will have to cope.
These days it's very easy
to sit around and mope
and long for all those days long gone
when we were free to walk,
to socialise, to shop, to work,
to meet family, to talk.

I find that I've slowed down a lot.
I used to rush about
and cram too much into my day
and never take time out.
But lockdown's given us a gift,
the time to stand and stare
to notice things around us,
appreciate, compare.

For England's just as beautiful
as any foreign land.
Our beaches sometimes stretch for miles,
all filled with golden sand.
The countryside is green and cool.
Our woods are free to roam.

Yes! I am learning that there really is
no place like home!

I've learned to value all I have,
my life, my friends, my health.
Add into that my family
and I have untold wealth.
I'll cope because I know, one day,
we all will be together
and my whole life will be complete.
Lockdown is NOT forever!

Hope

Yes!! Now we've had our vaccines!
I'm not frightened any more.
A big weight has been lifted.
I'm safe and I'm secure.
I'm filled with hope that we will
all be free to live again.
For all of us have to admit
this year has been a strain.
But we have fought and we've survived,
helped others when we could,
obeyed the rules and tried to smile
each day to lift the mood.
We've cherished our surroundings.
We've valued all our friends,
been supported by our families,
accepted what life sends.

We're lucky that we're pensioners.
An income is assured.
We've not missed travelling so much,
too old to go abroad?
We have our homes. We have our health.
We really can't complain.
But OH! how lovely it will be
to hug our sons again!
To see them in the flesh instead

of faces on the screen.
That day is nearly here, I hope,
the BEST there's ever been!
And I'VE learned to appreciate
the gifts that fill my life.
I hope I'm now a better friend,
grandma and mum and wife.

Brisk

I came across a word today
which set my brain a thinking.
The word was 'brisk',
my poor old heart was seriously sinking!
How long ago is it since 'brisk'
could be applied to me?
Some months ago, I fear,
but then I thought 'why should that be?'
In Lockdown I have slowed right down.
I cook and clean and talk,
but then I just meander
when I take my daily walk.

SO

I gave myself a talking to.
My new buzz word is 'brisk'.
I've gathered pace when climbing stairs
and round the house I whisk!
I've upped my speed when walking.
I do my exercises.
I'm determined to get fit again,
to drop at least two sizes!
How strange that such a little word
can change my life this way.
(I'm hoping that my buzz word lasts
for more than just one day!)

Meandering!

Meander is my favourite word.
It conjures up the days
when we have time to wander round
and we have time to gaze
upon the beauty all around,
to breathe in the fresh air,
to wonder at the miracles
of nature everywhere.

Rivers and streams meander too.
They flow towards the sea
in never ending movement,
just like LIFE for you and me.
For when they meet an obstacle,
they find a way around it
until the route ahead is clear.
It's theirs once they have found it.

Sometimes their path is rocky
and nothing can be done
but gather strength and battle through
until the way is won.

C19's been a rocky road
for all of us this year.
We've also battled through and soon
the way ahead WILL clear.

Two Sides to Every Story

The fox came down our garden
I love to see him there
investigating all around.
Stopping to sniff the air.
Some people feed the foxes
and I can understand.
I'm privileged to watch
these feral creatures close at hand.

BUT

they have a nasty habit.
They mark their territory!
It kills my plants and leaves a stench
although it's only wee.

THEN, this last year my hair's grown long.
It's growing naturally
and I have left it just to be
the style it wants to be.
I don't wake up and think
'What outfit should I wear today?'
I don the same old comfy clothes.
I'm ready for my day.
My face is free of make-up.
I don't look very glam!

For no one's going to see me,
and I am what I am.

Two sides to every story,
it's very plain to see
for I have found, in Lockdown,
the FREEDOM to be me!

Hot Water

It's been so cold these last few days.
I've snuggled down at night
with my hot water bottle,
its stopper screwed down tight.
Such joy, then, to get into bed.
Sometimes too hot, but mostly
I love it 'cos it keeps my toes
and feet all warm and toasty.

Hot water is a useful thing
we often take for granted.
For our machines and dishwashers
it's all we ever wanted.
For hot baths full of bubbles,
warm showers every day
and lazing in a hot tub
(if one should come our way!)

BUT THEN there is the other sort,
the kind that means there's trouble,
intruding on our peaceful lives
and bursting our safe bubbles.
I want to find solutions,
to work the problems out.
For what's the point in getting cross
and throwing things about?

Let's talk, discuss together,
to find the right way through,
for surely that would be the most
productive thing to do.

Hot water's such a blessing,
but, you know, the best for me,
is when the water's boiling
for a nice hot cup of tea!

A Spring in my Step

The garden's full of snowdrops.
The cyclamen abound.
The daffodils are all in bud.
There's promise all around.
And I can start to plant my seeds,
to watch them grow and sprout
and in a few weeks they will be
just right for planting out.

Now some days will be sunny.
There's freshness in the air
and on our walks, we'll see that buds
are forming everywhere.
The birds are singing lustily.
They're looking for a mate.
Camelias are flowering
and I am feeling great.

Then, just TODAY, amazing news!
A plan to set us free!
How wonderful for us
return to normal life will be!
The whole world's learned from Lockdown.
There's a smile upon my face,
for I have hope that now our world
will be a better place!

As Old as you Feel

'You're as old as you feel' – it's a well-known line
and I use it a lot now I'm seventy-nine.

Some days I can't quite get it into my head
when inside I'm twelve, but my legs feel like lead.

I know I can giggle and dance all about
but just moments later my hips will give out.

I start off to walk for a few miles or more
but after ten minutes my knees are so sore.

I know I can climb flights of stairs to the top
but before I get halfway my breathing just stops.

I know I can swim for an hour or more
but fifteen lengths later I'm heading for shore.

Yes, I feel so healthy and lively inside
and I'm still enjoying this life's bumpy ride
and there's one thing I know
that will NEVER wear out
that's my love for the people that I care about!

Deliveries

At first, it was a nightmare.
We couldn't get a slot.
We used up all the store cupboard,
the freezer, all we'd got.
But how it's changed!
Deliveries can now be any time
and any day! We're really spoiled.
The choice is yours or mine.

It's a real highlight in our week.
It's service with a smile,
a friendly chat, a helping hand.
They go the extra mile.
And we are saving money!
We're just buying what we need.
We don't snap up the two for one's
or chocolate.
(No more greed!)

So when this lockdown's over
and we are free again,
will we go shopping every week
or will it be a pain?
It surely is a blessing,
this shopping at the door.

So will we never visit
supermarkets anymore?

We'll keep our slot though. Sometimes
we like browsing round the shelves,
so we'll still shop for top ups
to choose things for ourselves.

AND

There's one BIG thing I hope
that will return for us sometime,
that's shopping in a clothes store,
no fun doing THAT online!

In Search Of Laughter

There's been a lack of laughter
in this last year or so
instead there have been many times
when tears begin to flow.
For everywhere is empty
and everywhere is quiet.
There's been no interaction,
no warmth to fill our hearts.

Sometimes TV can raise a smile,
but there are very few
programmes that make me chuckle.
(Like "Would I lie to you?")
In facetimes with our families
we search for things to say
to make us laugh a little,
to cheer each other's day.

Like yesterday, a blood test
and my blood pressure too.
I was so glad to see the nurse,
I chatted as I do.
We laughed together when we saw
her efforts were in vain
and I had to STOP TALKING
to do blood pressure again.

And often I just never know
where my glasses can be.
I put them down beside me,
but know with certainty
they'll be somewhere inside the house,
on table, bed or chair
and once even inside the fridge!
I find them anywhere.

We do strange things when getting old.
I try to laugh, not care
when I put coffee in my cup
and find a teabag there.
And so it all comes down to this,
I'm laughing at myself.
I try to see the funny side.
It's better for my health!

BUT

From the first of April
when we CAN meet face to face,
That's when I know my laughter
will be permanently in place!

It's Magic!

I bought a bunch of daffodils,
that's what the label said!
Some long green stems
with little papery bags upon each head.
I popped them in some water,
soon the bags began to split,
by bedtime we saw yellow!
(Just a little bit.)
The morning showed the buds all swelled,
at least four times their size.
By lunchtime petals could be seen,
unfurled before our eyes,
then orange trumpets!
Soon the vase was filled with gorgeous blooms!
I recommend some daffodils to brighten ALL our rooms.

Touch Wood

No! I'm not superstitious,
but I don't like tempting fate
and so I'll leave a cake
if it's the last one on the plate.
I don't walk under ladders,
pass someone on the stair,
I uncross knives when people
leave them lying, unaware.

I like to see two magpies,
for one alone means sorrow.
I search round for his partner,
to safeguard my tomorrow.
When small I never stepped upon
the joins in paving stones.
(But now I rarely jump along,
in case I break my bones!)

Black cats will always bring us luck.
Bird poo? I'm not so keen.
Odd numbers are the lucky ones,
unless it is thirteen!
I'm always optimistic
that good things will come once more.
(But I look around for wood to touch,
that way I'm DOUBLY sure!)

A Switchback Ride

The first few days of April have been
like a switchback ride!
At last we saw our family,
though it had to be outside.
I can't describe the moment
when I saw them all for real.
Oh! How they've grown! How wonderful
to talk and share a meal
and catch up on the last few months,
enjoy their company,
to laugh and be together.
How happy it made me!
Then Sunday we could visit
our younger son and wife,
enjoy their lovely garden
and catch up with their lives,
to share some fun and happiness,
some gorgeous Easter gifts.
A special day. A sunny day.
It gave us such a lift!

But soon there came the downward slope,
a sudden frightful shock.
One of life's problems from outside.
Our family is our rock.

A gradual climb back up again,
the blossom flourishing.
Then overnight a short sharp frost
which damaged everything.

But look, some buds are still in bloom.
There's still beauty to share
and nature gives us hope once more,
that we are nearly there.

'Til Friday brought us such sad news.
Our 'Grand Old Duke' has died.
Once more we're on the downward path
and our whole country cries.

BUT, we'll be strong! We'll hold on tight.
This ride is temporary.
We'll soon be free and we'll consign
this year to memory.

(I think I prefer the roundabout!)

Housework

Oh no! It's Thursday morning
and it is cleaning day!
I've got to do the housework,
but I want to go and play
inside my little greenhouse,
seedlings need to be pricked out
and everything is growing.
It's all starting to sprout!
But I have to do the housework
and it takes a bit of time.
I hoover, dust, and polish
and soon it will look fine.
So THEN I will escape into
the garden in the sun!
Yes, housework is a chore
but it looks lovely when it's done!

Itchy Feet!

Hooray! I've tasted freedom!
Now I've got itchy feet!
I want to rush back into life,
explore and meet and greet,
join friends inside a country pub
where someone else has cooked,
have something to look forward to,
a holiday we've booked?

What bliss to meet with loved ones
anywhere in sun or rain,
for we can go inside
and be together once again.
I want to see a film or show,
enjoy a blissful swim
and meet up at the bridge club
and get my hair a trim!

Just to be free will be so good,
enjoy a special treat
without having to dodge around
the people that we meet.

I don't want to waste a moment.
We've survived an awful year.
Now we can face the future
with full steam and in top gear!

My Hairdresser

Of all the special people
we have missed most in Lockdown,
hairdressers must be near the top,
they surely wear the crown
for helping us to look our best,
to face the world each day,
for building up our courage
to set forth into the fray.

But through the isolation months,
our locks have grown apace.
For me, when I lean forward,
no one can see my face!
Some look like Wurzel Gummidge,
some are like Charles 1st,
some have big curls or bushy hair.
We all look at our worst.

But wait! There's an advantage!
I can have a ponytail!
I don't spend ages curling
my straight hair to no avail.
I've had time to experiment,
grown fond of my new hair,
so easy to look after,
just wash and brush, I'm there!

Fiona has worked wonders,
she shaped my hair so well
that even though it's much too long,
no one can really tell.
So, I'm going to seize the moment!
I'll keep my youthful style
'til someone tells me I'm too old,
then I'll cut it with a smile.

Upcycling!

I watched a program on TV,
an old, brown, wooden chest
of drawers. The presenter
just fell on them with zest!
I'll make them look so special!
I'll bring them up to date!
I'll transform them! You'll desire them!
Well, I just couldn't wait.
She sanded them. She papered them.
She filled in the odd crack.
She added shiny handles.
She really had the knack.
They looked so different with new paint,
(though still the same old lump).
They now had a new lease of life.
She'd saved them from the dump!

   WELL

Lockdown's done the same for me,
it's rubbed off my sharp bits.
I see my life with different eyes
and I am pleased it fits!
I'm happy now with simple things,
not striving as before
and everything's a bonus!

I appreciate life more.
I'm different from the inside out.
I don't mind how I look
for this is me and life's too short.
I'm like an open book.
So though I've gained a bit of weight,
I have a different view.
I'm confident because INSIDE
I've been upcycled too!

Gardeners

We've all turned into gardeners!
We tend our little plots,
We grow things in our flowerbeds.
We grow things in our pots.
And some of us are amateurs
and some of us are pros
and all the time we make mistakes,
but everything still grows.

There are some funny moments too
like growbags for example.
My friend bought two and brought them home
and couldn't wait to sample
her crop of fresh tomatoes!
But they seemed to have such thirst,
for what she hadn't realized
was she had to plant some first!

My aunt received an orchid.
A truly, lovely plant.
She watered it so carefully
with all that it could want.
But sadly, it just stayed the same.
It didn't want to grow.
'Til one day someone told her,
It's a silk one. Did you know?

But best, we recommended
chicken pellets, great for feed.
Just sprinkle on the borders.
They're all that your plants need.
My friends told me
'The chicken NUGGETS
really worked a treat!'
We laughed so much,
the foxes would have all
that they could eat!

Yes, gardening's frustrating
when the snails eat all our greens,
huge caterpillars chomp along,
blackfly infest the beans,
the slugs destroy the hostas,
there's black spot on the rose
and pesky weeds grow everywhere
as every gardener knows.

But the miracles of nature
are there for us to see
and our small havens are
one of the best places to be.
I think of you relaxing
in your happy outside space,
surrounded by your flowers
with a big smile on your face!

Daisies

There's nothing quite so cheerful
as a daisy in the grass.
Its perky little face seems
to be smiling as you pass.
The perfect white against the green,
and flourishing all round
a multitude of daisies,
all sprinkled on the ground.

It makes me smile to see them
proudly raised up to the sun.
All formed with such perfection,
every single one.
With memories of daisy chains,
of laughter, peace and rest,
I know, of all life's pleasures,
the simplest are the best!

PART III

I'm 80!

> "It's not how old you are,
> but how you are old"
>
> Jules Renard

It's never too late!

For goodness sake, I'm nearly 80,
so, what have I been doing lately?
Well, all my life I've written rhymes
for birthdays, weddings, special times
and commented about this life
while being mum and nan and wife.

But getting old just made me think.
Well, I could just sit here and sink
and get all sad and look a sight,
but why don't I stand up and fight
and just enjoy it while I'm here?
(Then Covid stepped me up a gear)

I looked for things that made me smile
and after just a little while
I had two books and now a third
of little rhymes no one has heard!
It's been such a fun thing to do.
I hope that you enjoy them too!

A Gold Star!!!

I sometimes got gold stars at school
if I was very good
and learned my spellings, did my sums
and all the things I should.
But since those days gold stars are few
and far between I fear.
When you grow up a gold star
is a thing of yesteryear.

For I'm not a top athlete
or a celebrity
and I don't own a big hotel.
No I am only me!
Gold stars are just a memory.
I'm happy where I am.
I don't think I deserve gold stars
for it would be a sham.
   YET
The best gold star in all my life
that there could EVER be
was on my 80th Birthday
when my family came to tea.
Our son opened their car boot
and there for me to see
was a great big golden star balloon
all shiny just for ME!!

Marital Bliss

My husband likes the lights up high,
I like them turned down low
for bright lights show up all my flaws
and make my wrinkles show.
I say to him "We're getting old.
I like a flattering glow!"
He says "I need a bright light 'cos I'm reading.
Don't you know?"
But STILL when I am passing,
I dim them as I go,
Geoff turns them up again
and it's a battle, to and fro!

I always have the volume
on the TV turned up loud
for all the actors mumble
and I can't hear a sound.
But Geoff can hear it all it seems.
"They'll hear it in the garden!"
and I remind him that it's dark
and then he says "Beg pardon?"
It's strange but on the evenings
when he goes first to bed
he'll turn it down, so I just turn it up
and shake my head.

We like to go for walks,
but Geoff walks fast and I walk slow.
His legs are long and mine are short,
I take more steps you know.
He waits for me to catch him up
but just as I arrive
he's off again! But I must catch
my breath to stay alive!
Yet, now we're old and find that we
are both using a stick.
Geoff's slowed a bit, I've speeded up
and now we're BOTH as quick!

Geoff likes to be at home,
he's quietly happy with his life.
I love to socialise and chat,
so there's a bit of strife.
So I'll stay home and he'll come out,
we've learned to compromise.
You'd think we're incompatible but
we're really the right size
and looking back over the years,
they couldn't have been finer
and I wouldn't swap my dear old man
for all the tea in China!

Catching Leaves

When we were young and walking
in the woods on autumn days
there was a very special game,
one that we always played.
The leaves were falling from the trees
and swirling round and round.
Our challenge was to catch one,
before it touched the ground.

But it's more tricky than it sounds!
Leaves dancing in the air
would dodge our hands, just out of reach
and fall just anywhere.
We'd twirl and twist, just like the leaves
and when we caught just one
we'd take it home — our lucky leaf!
and it was so much fun.

(and I STILL do it today, whenever I can!
I'm so happy when I catch one!)

Autumn

I woke to a beautiful autumn day,
with pale, wispy clouds just drifting away,
the promise of sunshine breaking through
and all over the grass the morning dew.
A million diamonds sparkling there.
A breathtaking sight in the fresh autumn air.

Autumn and harvest, the season of wealth,
when we gather produce to store on the shelf.
The fruit in the orchards, the crops and the wheat,
for wildlife and humans there's plenty to eat.
A whole year's life cycle brings forth such reward.
Provisions for winter. A much needed hoard.

I, too, am in autumn, for I'm growing old,
with most of my life story already told.
MY fruits are my family. MY crops are my friends.
MY harvest the memories and blessings life sends.
So I'LL wear bright colours, put on a display
and celebrate autumn!
and even MAKE HAY!!

Senior Moments

Today, I lost my credit card
when I went out to lunch!
I bought myself a coffee with
a small biscuit to crunch
while waiting for my friends to come.
They're such a lovely bunch.
Then we perused the menu for
delicious food to munch.

BUT!!

Wherever is my credit card?
Perhaps it's by the till?
Or on the floor or in my coat?
I'll find it soon! I WILL!!
I search through every pocket.
I'm panicking, but still
my lovely Dianne rescued me
and kindly paid my bill.

I'm frantic and I'm worried.
I can't relax. I'm tense.
I used it here, but now it's gone!
It really makes no sense.
THEN!!
It's in my trouser pocket!

I really am so dense
and 'ANOTHER senior moment!'
is my only defence.

Just one of many lately.
Please say you have them too?
I'm always just forgetting things
and losing things. Do you?
I put things away safely
but then they move! It's TRUE!
(But how they do it on their own
I just don't have a clue!)

Colours

We all love wearing colours.
They brighten up our day
and they can show the mood we're in
and what we want to say.
Some days when I was working,
I needed to wear red,
a sign of strength and confidence
helped face the day ahead.

At weekends it was often green,
just like our natural world,
for calm and relaxation
as my precious time unfurled
and I would then enjoy
the coming hours at my leisure
and fill them up with all the things
that really gave me pleasure.

When I was young, I always liked
to wear the colour blue.
A simple colour, clean and fresh,
and hopeful, pure and true.
The colour of the sky above,
the colour of the sea,
with all the promise of
a happy day ahead for me.

But, now I'm old, I find that
I like yellow more and more.
It's such a joyful colour
and I can't be sad for sure.
For when I'm wearing yellow,
I want to sing and dance
and say, 'I'M HERE!' –'I'M STILL ALIVE!'
I'm taking every chance
to celebrate, enjoy my life
with friends and family,
for EVERY day's a bonus
and that's good enough for me!

Socks!!!

Geoff's pink sock may LOOK normal,
but it's got special powers!
It's always playing silly tricks
and hides away for hours.
There's always one sock missing
when I empty the machine
and it's ALWAYS the pink one!
It must be caught between
the rugby shirts and sweaters.
I'll find it soon I know,
so in the tumble drier this laundry load will go.

It's all dry now. I fold the clothes
and shake the tea towels out
but when I pair the socks all up,
the pink one's not about!
I've found it in the rain outside.
I've found it on the stair.
I've found it in the laundry basket.
Did I leave it there?
I've found it in MY sock drawer.
I've found it on a shelf!
It makes me wonder,
did I somehow put it there myself?
I've really got quite cross with it.
I've tried to use my brain

by fastening two together,
but they just come loose again.
The other socks behave themselves
but this one is a trial.
So when, at last, it shows itself
I break into a smile!

I've only noticed this strange thing
in the last month or two,
so now I've got a cunning plan!
I know just what I'll do!!
I'll HIDE the pink socks right down
at the bottom of the drawer
and Geoff won't even wear them!
So I'll have WON for sure!

BUT

next wash day

Oh No! There's one sock missing!
I've got just ONE that's green!
Can you believe the other one
is nowhere to be seen????

Tough!

In life there will be times when
we must face the things ahead,
a meeting or appointment that
fills our hearts with dread,
that causes sleepless nights,
although there's nothing we can do.
That time will always come around,
so how can we get through?
And often things turn out to be
much better than we thought,
so this is what I try to do
before I get too fraught.

I try to focus on TODAY,
at what is happening NOW.
I look for a small treat
(that's if my diet will allow!)
I watch TV or read a book
to occupy my mind.
I busy myself doing jobs,
just anything I find.
But after all my efforts,
if I'm STILL feeling sick,
I've found a timely glass of wine
will always do the trick!

An Uncertain World

The beginning of December.
Can we anticipate
a Christmas with our families?
That would be really great.
Our world is so uncertain.
It's hard to look ahead.
Let's just live in the moment.
Let's enjoy NOW instead.
Be grateful for the morning,
for waking up each day,
for food and warmth and shelter,
although skies may be grey.
There's always something special,
if you look hard enough,
to cheer your heart and give you strength
when life is getting tough.
Let's smile and spread some sunshine
in all the things we do,
for if YOU share some happiness,
it will bounce back to you.

Whistling!

I was thinking about whistling
just the other day.
Such a happy, cheerful sound
we've lost along the way.
I used to wake each morning
to the milkman on his round,
his cheerful whistle spreading smiles
as he clinked the bottles down.

The postman always whistled too
as he popped the letters through.
Men whistled on their way to work…
a happy thing to do.
Yes, all those years ago we
seemed a real community
and people loved to whistle
at each opportunity.

One note is all that I can do,
though I try with all my might
but our son can whistle ANY tune
and it's a real delight!
It lifts the heart and cheers me up
and makes me smile and so
I challenge you! Put down your phone
and WHISTLE as you go!

Crackers!!

I'm crackers for everything Christmas,
the bright decorations, the tree,
the cards plopping through on the doormat,
the fir, mistletoe and holly,
the mince pies, mulled wine, Christmas puddings,
the yule log and rich Christmas cake,
but, above all, I lOVE Christmas crackers
and the lovely big SNAP that they make!

I know they're a big waste of money,
just cardboard and paper and tat
and everyone groans at the terrible jokes
and it's only me wearing a hat!
But it's still fun to pull them & see what's inside,
even if it's a curly up fish,
'cos when we're all there round the table and happy
it's then that I make my BIG wish.

HEALTH, WEALTH and HAPPINESS
EVERYONE!!

The Magic of Christmas.

I wish you a magical Christmas,
like the ones we had when we were young
before the commercialisation,
the waste and the greed had begun.
We knew the true meaning of Christmas.
The wonderful Nativity.
When sharing and being together
and kindness and love were the key.
I remember once, I was an angel,
with wings that were larger than me
and we went carol singing in a tuneful group
holding lanterns so that we could see.
The weeks before Christmas were busy.
Not shopping as we do today
for there was no money, we had to make do
and we had lots of fun on the way.
With lavender bags for the aunties,
a hankie embroidered for gran
and hand knitted scarves for my sister and mum
and fingerless gloves for a man,
we knitted and sewed, made peppermint creams
and mince pies and puddings and cake
and paperchains festooned our ceilings,
with intricate cut out snowflakes.

We had a small tree in the window,
with tinsel and cottonwool snow,
no lights but real candles and when they were lit,
they set our small faces aglow.
They only burned for a few minutes.
Those moments were so magical.
As we sat there watching the flickering flames,
we drank in the wonder, enthralled.
I still have the celluloid angel,
who stood at the top of the tree.
We don't use her now, she's too fragile,
for she's getting old, just like me.
There were a few presents, a Christmas day tea,
with aunties and grandmas and all
and then a great singsong with laughter and jokes
and I sang although I was small.

And Christmas is still such a magical time
to share life with family and friends.
Let's spread love and kindness and laughter
and hope for the future as '21 ends!

My New Year Resolution

The turkey is eaten, the carols are sung
the gifts given out and received.
It's all over again and some may be sad
but some will be very relieved!

A new year is coming. We'll make resolutions
to regroup and make a fresh start.
Let's all think of others, be kind to our friends
and give of ourselves from the heart.

If we're lucky in life, we'll all have a person
to cheer us when we're in the dumps.
This year I'LL try hard to be one of those people
and hope I sometimes come up trumps.

Let's all hope for a better year in 2022

Toilet Humour

There was a toilet in Cabbage Key
and it had just a flap for a door
and we could all see my friend's face and her feet.
(but thankfully, not any more!)
We doubled up laughing 'til it was our turn,
pulling faces and teasing each other,
I'll never forget the fun we all had
AND how grateful. (There wasn't another!)

In Venice we found just a hole in the floor.
Should I back in or face straight ahead?
Then the time when we patiently queued in a line
but one lady went straight in instead!
Today there were three in a space made for two
and one of us was rather stout
but we chatted and laughed while we waited
and then did a dance to get out!

Let's all share the stories that made us all smile
for it's something we do every day
and I am so grateful to one Thomas Crapper
for now we can flush it away!

All of a Twist!

It's strange as I get older.
I'm always writing lists
for EVERYTHING or else, I find,
I'm getting in a twist!

Just little things like getting
next day's meal out of the freezer
or what we'll have for dinner,
well that will be a teaser.
It's fish and chips again!
Oh well! My Geoff won't make a fuss
for even after all these years,
that's still a treat for us!

I write lists in the morning
of things that I must do,
like phone calls, thank you's, bills to pay.
Oh dear, some housework too.
And then there is my shopping list.
It's always on the wall
so I can add things day by day
and don't forget it all.

My calendar's so useful,
for it's my daily chart,
appointments (Yes, they're multiplying

as I fall apart!).
And good things too like visits
from family and friends
and great days out and games of bridge,
whatever else life sends.

I have a little notebook
which I carry round with me
to jot down names and places,
to aid my memory.
When people tell me things, I'm finding
that they go straight through.
"In one ear out the other",
my mum said and it's so true!

It's strange but in most homes these days
there are no lists in sight
'cos mobile phones and laptops
keep THEIR lives working right.
I'm SAFE with pen and paper.
Those things give me a fright,
so I'll write my last list today
and I'll sleep well tonight!

Funny Habits

I have some funny habits.
I'm sure that you do too
for in this stressful life of ours
they help to get us through!!

I bought some coloured pegs today,
pink, yellow, green and blue
and when I hang my washing out,
one thing I always do.
I match pegs to each item,
pink to pink and green to green.
They look so perky hanging there,
so colourful and clean!

I'm strange in other ways as well,
when eating toast, I've found
it tastes much more delicious
when I eat the wrong way round.
I turn it upside down so that
the spread is on my tongue
and all the flavour fills my mouth!
Just try it everyone!

I found a special pebble,
it's only very wee.
It looks just like a guinea pig,

comes everywhere with me.
I put it in my pocket,
that day two years ago
and its my lucky pebble!
(Don't ask me how I know!)

Please tell me that you're just like me
and have peculiar ways!
They make us who we are
and can add laughter to our days,
for if you share them with your friends,
they'll share their foibles too
and you will find, to your relief,
that it's NOT only you!

A Silver Lining

I really love my little car,
so much a part of me.
I've owned it now for 15 years.
It's getting old you see.
Some bits are starting to wear out
and I know how it feels
even though I've got two legs
and it's just got four wheels.

The other day, as we drove home,
a warning light appeared,
another, then another!
This is the END we feared!
We struggled on. The steering went.
Geoff coaxed it to the side,
a safe layby, just off the road.
"Come on, old friend, I cried".

Then, dashing to the rescue,
our hero in his van,
the AA man called Michael,
the most amazing man.
He knew exactly what it was,
and in an hour or two,
a new fan belt was fitted
and my car was good as new!

And there WAS a silver lining,
for we weren't towed away.
We didn't have a garage bill
with V A T to pay!
We helped him back – a tasty tip,
our feedback was top rate
for it could have been disaster
but we drove home feeling great!

So many things that happen
can be viewed in different ways.
We CAN look on the black side,
but it leads to gloomy days.
"Look for the silver lining"
my lovely mum told me.
"Sometimes you have to dig quite deep,
but you WILL find one. You'll see".

A brighter way of dealing with
the obstacles in life.
A shift to look for positives
when you're up to here with strife.
Your glass half full, a rainbow,
a message that you've missed.
Look for the silver lining
and become an optimist!

Dining with Friends

It's always a fun evening
when friends come round to dine.
We chat and laugh, enjoying
delicious food and wine.
We talk of our experiences
and share the latest news.
We like to set the world to rights.
We all have different views.
We talk until the cows come home,
until they're in their sheds
and often it's past midnight
when at last we seek our beds.

But have you noticed how we've changed
throughout the last few years?
We're on the wine and gin now,
no longer drinking beers.
We often have a takeaway,
so no one has to cook.
We rarely play pop music,
we now discuss our books.
We all have strong opinions,
so politics are banned
'cos it sometimes gets quite rowdy
and can get out of hand!

We aim for happy evenings,
so world news is forbidden.
We feel so bad for everyone
at war but keep it hidden.
There's one more subject that's taboo,
discussing medication!
To listen to each other's ailments
takes some dedication!
We realized how times had changed
one evening, one by one
we sat and took our blood pressures,
has this become our fun??
                BUT
In spite of all the topics
we no longer talk about,
we still have brilliant evenings,
of that there is no doubt.
We talk about our lives, our thoughts,
the things that make us grin,
the food we like, a TV show,
the state our minds are in!
We talk about our past adventures
(those we can remember!)
We have so much to share that
we could chat until December!

Sweet Peas

I picked the first sweet pea today
and breathed in its perfume,
so breath-taking, miraculous,
its scent could fill a room.

No one could ever replicate
the perfume of a flower
although they mix and blend and tweak
for hour after hour.
Not lily of the valley,
not freesias or a rose,
not stocks or honeysuckle,
we can't manufacture those.

To wander in a garden
as the perfume fills the air
in awe of the perfection
of each flower everywhere,
the wonders of our natural world
displayed for all to see,
to stop, to breathe, appreciate,
that's paradise to me.

Shades of Green

I was lucky to visit a garden today
and I sat on a bench in the sun
and I gazed at the trees
and the shrubs and the grass
and they were all green, every one.
BUT each green was different,
some light and some dark
and all variations between.
I just hadn't realized in all my long life,
there are so many shades of green!

And I thought, it's like people.
We live on this planet.
We make up the whole human race
and WE all need water
and food and sunlight
and to live in a warm and safe place.
WE want to be happy,
to flourish and grow
for inside we all feel the same.

But our lives are so different
and I'm praying daily
for peace in our world once again.

Stuck!

I do admire designers
with ingenious inventions.
To protect our children (and ourselves)
from harm is their intention.
But now I'm getting older,
I find that their solutions
just make life HARDER
so I'm going to start a revolution!

                PLEASE!

No more ring pulls on my cans
or even my sardines.
No tiny pills in bubbles.
No keys on corned beef tins.
No stuck down tops on milk bottles.
No childproof bottled bleach.
For my old fingers just can't press
or squeeze or pull on each.

And I can't open bottles
(though I CAN manage wine!)
but jars of sauce or pickles,
they really are a sw—nuisance.
I find I have to plan ahead
'til a friendly face comes by.

Oh, how I miss my milkman,
he was such a helpful guy.

And I'm in mortal danger!
I attack with sharpened blade.
If it should slip I'll stab myself,
a goner I'm afraid.
So if YOU'RE a designer
and you want to save a life
PLEASE invent an opener
that doesn't cause me strife!

Bring Me Sunshine!

To wake up in the morning
with the sunlight shining through,
the promise of another day,
no matter what we do.
I'm filled with smiles and happiness
as I leap out of bed.
('til I remember that I'm old
and my legs feel like lead).

But never mind, my time's my own,
each moment is a treasure
and I can revel in the warmth,
enjoy it at my leisure.
I phone a friend, invite them round
for biscuits cake and tea.
The sunshine, food and friendship,
that's good enough for me.

And everywhere are people smiling,
lifted by the sun.
A jaunty step, a joyful face.
"Good morning, everyone!"
Forget about the rainy days,
the cold, the frost, the mist.
It's great to be in England
on a sunny day like this.

And I have found throughout my life
a SMILE is like the sun.
I'm on a mission to spread
happiness to every one.
For what's the point in frowning?
It makes people feel bad,
so I will smile at everyone
even if you think I'm mad!

Phones!!!

Yes, now I'm getting on a bit,
the world's a scary place
for everybody walks round with
a phone against their face.
They're isolated in a
little bubble of their own,
so even if they're in a crowd,
they're really all alone!

The world's become dependent
on new technology
but we are from a different time
and it's a mystery.
We find it hard to learn new things.
We WANT to stay in touch
with facetimes, email, messages,
but we find it a bit much!

One of my friends has got a phone,
its tiny, pink and plastic,
a children's phone, the ringtone moos or clucks,
it's just fantastic!
She only needs to make a call
to show she's still around.
It's all she wants. She finds it suits
her right down to the ground!

Another has a tiny phone.
She got it years ago
and she has never changed it,
it's great, pay as you go.

BUT I wanted a NEW phone
and it's fraught with difficulty.
Transferring all the data's
an anathema to me.
I've phoned for help and guidance.
I really want to win
but I need a private tutor
or I'll throw it in the bin!

It used to be so satisfying
phoning up a friend
and listening to their disembodied
voice upon the end.
First we'd find a phone box,
make sure we had some change,
then we'd all squeeze in together,
all within hearing range.
We'd lift the big receiver
to hear the connect tone
then DIAL in all the numbers.
It was called a "Dog and Bone".

NOW, I'm hopeless with technology.
It's not that I've forgotten
but I was taught to write and spell
not how to press a BUTTON!

(Thank goodness – after a lot of help and 10 days later I know how to use it!)

Lambs!!!

We've just got back from Devon
and the sun shone all the while.
Based on the edge of Exmoor,
we drove and walked for miles
exploring ancient villages,
just like a picture book
with daffodils and primroses
banked everywhere we looked.

And every field was FULL of lambs.
Such an amazing sight.
Some were brindled, some were black,
some mixed but mainly white.
We stopped to watch them gambolling.
I thought they were so sweet
'til my friend said "they're jumping
'cos the grass tickles their feet!"

How lucky we've all been this week,
the first few days of spring.
Flowers are bursting into bloom
and trees are blossoming.
This year especially the spring seems
brighter than before
and I'll say thank you every day
while I pray for those at war…

A Moment in the Sun

The irises are over,
they make such a display,
their beauty so breath-taking,
before they fade away.
This year, the rhododendrons
were full of glorious blooms,
I even put some in a vase
to brighten up our room.
The peonies all flourished,
the whole garden seemed to say
"This spring's a celebration
and we're still here. Hooray!!"

It's sad, though, that these glorious blooms
just last for a few weeks.
They wait all year and then they bloom
a short while at their peaks.
But, maybe, we appreciate
their beauty even more.
If their blooms were perpetual,
would they become a bore?
Like everything in life,
we value those things that are rare.
No one would value DIAMONDS
if they were everywhere!

When I look back, I treasure
MY moments in the sun,
adventures, an experience,
some things that I have done.
I had to wait 'til 80
to achieve THIS special time
and I still can't believe that
people like to share my rhymes!
So let us all appreciate
OUR moments in the sun.
(And I can vouch its not too late
to enjoy another one!).

The Beach

A Sunday School trip to the seaside
and we always swam, rain or shine,
built sandcastles, wrapped ourselves up in a towel
and pretended the weather was fine.
We laid back and listened to waves coming in
and paddled our feet in the foam.
We ate sandy sandwiches and an ice cream
and then we sang all the way home!

There were days in a caravan down by the beach
when our boys were so young and so free,
with treasures like seaweed and pebbles and shells
and they were like seals in the sea!
Then came foreign lands and sunbeds with shades
and eating sardines in a shack.
We collected small stones just like jewels for a jar
with a candle for when we got back.
    (We've still got it!)

Well, now we are old and we still love the sea
though it's getting to be a rare treat
but we found ourselves down on Pevensey beach
where the pebbles were hurting our feet!
We still managed a paddle, then sat in the sun
but it was such a trial to get back
for the stones were so steep, I kept slipping down

'til Geoff found that he had the knack!
He held his umbrella, so I grabbed the end
and he hauled me up all in one go.
Well, we must have looked a hilarious sight,
but hopefully no one will know!

It's strange how some days last a lifetime
and others go by in a flash.
So I'll have adventures each day that I can.
(There's one waiting! So now I must dash!)

Help!!!

(Begin quietly and slowly getting faster, louder and panicky until STOP!!)

Do you ever wake up
and the day starts off all wrong?
You can't locate your glasses,
they're not where they belong.
You're running late, you really want to
read your book in bed
but a hospital appointment
is looming up ahead

and then, oh no, the milk's run out
so you drink your coffee black
and the cupboard door's left open
so you give your knee a whack
and the flowers are all wilting
for we badly need some rain
and it's much too hot to cook so
we'll have salad yet again

and the government seems useless
and it's costing more for less
and there's queues at all the airports
and the world is in a mess
and,

STOP!!!

Cheer up! Find your glasses.
Make some peanut buttered toast
and let's look on the bright side…
there's a letter in the post!
AN ADVERT FOR A STAIR LIFT??!!
Well, that's something I can cheer,
I CAN still climb the stairs and raise a smile
and I'M STILL HERE!!

So I'm counting all my blessings
and I'm living for each day
and I'm dancing round the room
'cos there's a song I love to play
whenever I am gloomy.
It always makes me smile
and it will do the same for you!
Just try it for a while.

DON'T WORRY! BE HAPPY!

(Thank you, Bobby McFerrin!!)

Feet!!

OUR feet are incredible
(though sometimes they're a trial!)
for in our lifetimes,
we will walk 100,000 miles!
That's THREE times round the world they say!
It's unbelievable,
but there it is in black and white,
it's irrefutable!

What would we do without them?
I truly value each,
even though, at my age,
they're sometimes hard to reach
and, sadly, they're beginning to
feel the worse for wear
with knobbly bits
and bunions appearing everywhere!

Our feet are not attractive,
some are bony, thin and long
and some are short and stubby
and some might even pong!!
Who'd pamper our feet every day?
An angel you'd have thought
for there are corns and fungus,
verrucas or a wart.

But here is my chiropodist!
All day they look at feet
and, somehow, they're among
the cheeriest people you could meet!
There's athlete's foot and blisters
and toenails and hard skin
but they don't seem to mind
the awful state our feet are in!

They gently scrape and soothe and rub
and chatter to us all
so we all feel that we could walk
the length of Hadrian's Wall!

So thank you all chiropodists,
for your kindness and your smiles,
for now we know our feet will last
for the last 2,000 miles!

Spiders!

What is it about spiders?
I shouldn't be afraid
but I am really spooked by them.
It's just the way they're made!
They can't help being ugly
but they're big and black and hairy.
It's their long legs.
They scuttle all about and they are scary!

I wouldn't mind if I was sure
that they would run and hide
but they're so unpredictable
and that I can't abide.
I see one come towards me
and I leap up and I'm gone!
I think the WORST thing is that
they just don't care where they run!

If I'm alone and one appears,
it's like facing a bear.
I run away and shout for help.
It's just my worst nightmare.
We all have spider stories,
like finding one in bed
or in our shoe or welli
or just above our head.

I'm never going to like them,
so I'll never live and thrive
for we all know that you should let
a spider run alive.
And even in the nursery rhyme,
Miss Muffet ran away!
I'm never going to change my feelings
now I'm old and grey.

I know that they're amazing.
Their webs are works of art
so delicate and beautiful,
so they're really very smart
        BUT
I'll collect my conkers
for they don't like the smell
and my house will be spider proof
and that's MY magic spell!

Pets

We used to have a parrot.
He was an African Grey.
He did so many tricks and he
learned lots of things to say.
He used to fly around our room
'til one day he escaped
and flew around the local trees
and people stood and gaped.
For he was calling "Hello Dear!"
and ringing like a phone
and whistling his favourite tune,
quite sad to be alone.
He stayed away for two whole days,
reported in the paper
then he flew home in search of food.
He'd had his little caper!

And we had fish and guinea pigs,
a hamster and a cat.
I'm sure you've had some favourite pets,
some odd ones too – a rat, a snake
or a tarantula, a hedgehog, or a mouse?
Some people have so many
there's no room inside their house!

They're so dependent on us for
their quality of life.
They comfort us when we're beset
with worries and with strife.
It's sad though, and its hard to cope
when our pets pass away
for they can't last as long as us.

BUT, maybe, there's a way
if you're like Derek,
for HE knows he'll never be alone
'cos he's made Benny's bark into
a ring tone on his phone.

Such a good idea Derek. Thank you.

Saying Goodbye

How hard it is to face the truth
that you're no longer there
to share our lives, to give a hug,
to show us that you care.
How will we cope without your smile,
the love you gave us all,
protecting us and always there
to catch us should we fall?

AND YET, we know that you will live
within our hearts each day.
We'll feel your presence guiding us
as we go on life's way.
You'll ALWAYS be a part of us,
those memories we made
are precious jewels and, like a diamond,
they will never fade.

So THANK YOU……(insert Name)……
from the very bottom of our hearts.
We'll smile because we know
that we will NEVER be apart.
We know you'll walk beside us
throughout the coming years
and everyday we'll think of you
with smiles instead of tears.

About the Author

Hello Everyone,

I'm Joyce and I'm now 81 years old. Over the past three years I've had such an adventure and I can't really believe it has happened to me!

Here is my book! Full of 101 rhymes for oldies like me! (and younger people who want to know what it's like!)

I've always written little rhymes for birthdays and celebrations, so when I reached my 78th birthday, I thought, I'm getting OLD, I'm going to write about how it feels and how I'm going to cope.

I shared my little poems with my family and friends, and they loved them and encouraged me to keep writing and I did! Soon I had books full of rhymes, so they encouraged me to even dare to publish them!

I've had so much fun writing them and sharing them at care homes, day centres and pensioner groups. I've met a lot of lovely people and we always have plenty of laughter and chat because they feel just the same!

I hope that you enjoy them too!

You can even find me on YouTube! (Search '78 and counting')
or email me at:
joyce@78andcounting.com

My favourite quote:

"The happiest people don't have the best of everything,
they make the best of everything they have"
Oprah Winfrey

Printed in Great Britain
by Amazon